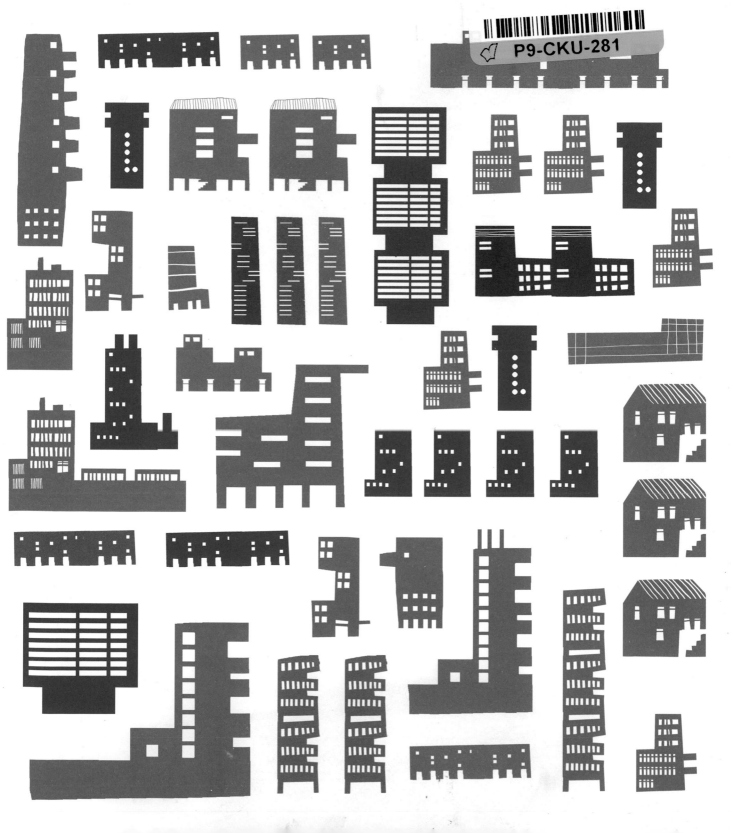

Text © 2008 Isabel Minhós Martins
Illustrations © 2008 Madalena Matoso
Translation © 2012 John Herring

Published in Portugal under the title *O Meu Vizinho é um Cão* © 2008
Planeta Tangerina, Carcavelos, Portugal
www.planetatangerina.com

Distributed in Canada by University of Toronto Press
5201 Dufferin Street, Toronto, Ontario M3H 5T8

Distributed in the United States by Publishers Group West
1700 Fourth Street, Berkeley, California 94710

Library and Archives Canada Cataloguing in Publication

Martins, Isabel Minhós
    My neighbor is a dog / written by Isabel Minhós Martins ;
illustrated by Madalena Matoso ; translated by John Herring.

Translation of: O meu vizinho e um cao.
ISBN 978-1-926973-68-5

    I. Matoso, Madalena II. Herring, John III. Title.

PZ7.M3685My 2013   j869.3'5   C2012-904070-3

Library of Congress Control Number: 2012943001

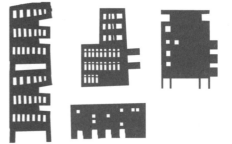

 Canadian Patrimoine
Heritage canadien

Canada

 Ontario
Ontario Media Development
Corporation

Canada Council Conseil des Arts
for the Arts du Canada

ONTARIO ARTS COUNCIL
CONSEIL DES ARTS DE L'ONTARIO

Société de développement
de l'industrie des médias
de l'Ontario

We acknowledge the financial support of the Canada Council for the Arts, the Ontario Arts Council, the Government
of Canada through the Canada Book Fund (CBF) and the Government of Ontario through the Ontario Media
Development Corporation's Book Initiative for our publishing activities.

Manufactured by WKT Co. Ltd.
Manufactured in Shenzhen, Guangdong, China, in September 2012
Job #12CB1186

A   B   C   D   E   F

owl kids Publisher of Chirp, chickaDEE and OWL
www.owlkidsbooks.com

My Neighbor Is a Dog

Isabel Minhós Martins

Madalena Matoso

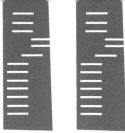

The building I lived in
was always very quiet.
Nothing ever happened there...

READY
MOVERS

Until one day a huge
moving truck pulled
up right in front of
our door...

All my neighbors went to their windows and saw large boxes, small boxes, tiny boxes—some in very strange shapes!

The next day,
our new neighbor
arrived...

He was a dog!

He barked a friendly "good morning" as he came in and then sat down on his porch to read the newspaper.

My parents thought it was very strange to have a dog as a neighbor.

They said he would leave his hair all over the stairs. That he'd hide bones in bizarre places. And that he'd scratch himself in a not-very-polite way.

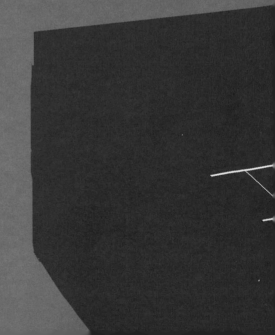

DAILY JOURNAL

STUDY:
Unsatisfied Neighbors

Results of a study confirm what has long been suspected: 76% of people do not like their neighbors and would gladly trade them.

It's a case of "my neighbor's neighbor is always nicer."

THE HOUSE OF YOUR DREAMS is already yours.

But I liked him.

I liked listening to him play his saxophone on the porch and watching him blow bubbles out of his candy-red pipe.

He was so friendly! He brought our newspaper to us every day.

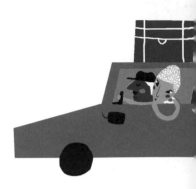

Soon another apartment in our building became empty.

And again another moving truck stopped in front of our door.

And once again we saw large boxes, small boxes, and tiny boxes appear. This time we also saw enormous boxes—some seemed almost intimidating!

**The next day,
the new neighbors arrived.**

**A couple of very
friendly elephants!**

My parents again found our new neighbors very strange.
They complained that their sheets took up too much space
on the clothesline, and something about the way they wrapped
their trunks around each other bothered them too.

I actually found them to be quite nice.

They helped me wash my father's car.
And in little time, they had washed all the cars in the neighborhood.
What's better than that?!

And then, once again, another apartment in our building became empty. And, once again, another moving truck pulled up outside our door.

All my neighbors gathered at their windows to see boxes, large, small, and tiny.

The new neighbor was very stylish.
I wondered if my parents would find him
to be a good neighbor.

It was late in the evening
when he arrived.

His yellow eyes shone in the dark
(as did his teeth, which showed
when he smiled).

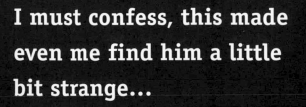

I must confess, this made
even me find him a little
bit strange...

But this feeling lasted
only a little while.
My crocodile neighbor was so nice
that he offered to teach me how to dance.

This past Christmas, he even dressed up as Santa Claus
and gave presents to everyone in the neighborhood: purses for
the ladies, shoes for the men, and for me, a tooth necklace.

My parents, though, rolled their eyes at him.

They said he was such a strange neighbor, and they sat in silence, sticking their tongues out at him.

So I asked my neighbors:

"Don't you find it strange that my parents find you strange?"

They immediately answered: "Your parents are the ones who are strange."

"They always look down on us," complained the dog.

"And always with their noses in the air," said the elephants.

"And they never even thanked me for my gifts," the crocodile said sadly.

And, you see, I had to agree. My neighbors deserved better neighbors!

I thought that I would talk to my parents,
but my mother was busy packing large boxes,
small boxes, tiny boxes...

"Oh!" I said. "Is someone else moving in?!"

The next day we moved out of our apartment
(and I should add: my neighbors and I were all very sad).

I heard that there were now three bears
living in our old apartment.
My old building was becoming more and
more fun to live in all the time...

And no wonder.

One day when I grow up,
I'm going to surprise my old neighbors.
I will stop in front of our old door with a
big moving truck...and I will move back in.

And I'm sure they won't find me strange!

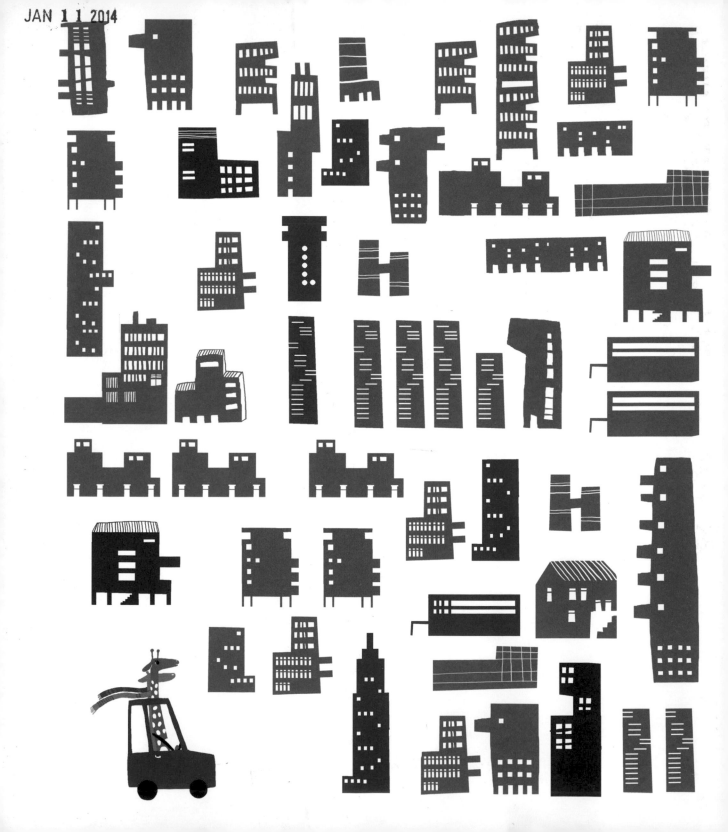